PEA-PLE OF THE WORLD

Written by
Melissa Mangiapanella

Illustrated by
Francesca Vitolo

ISBN: 978-1-63649-628-3

Library of Congress Control Number: 2020918024

Images by Francesca Vitolo.
Book Design by Travis D. Peterson.

Printed by IngramSpark, in the United States of America.

First printing edition 2020.

Melissa Mangiapanella
NY, New York
MelissaDMangiapanella@gmail.com

Pea-ple of the World

A loosely poetic children's book
redefining the stereotypical family structure.

To my husband, my best friend,
my pea-ce.

This book belongs to:

Little Pea, little Pea,

don't shed a tear.

families come in all
shapes and sizes, my dear.

Here's a pea mom, a pea dad,
sister and brother pea too.
But what completes

a loving family

is little pea, you.

This mommy here
does it all on her own.
In her little pea castle,
she sits on her throne.

But what does she have
that matches the rest?
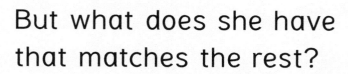
that comes from her chest.

This little pea lives
with his uncle and aunt.
They are always by his side and

never let him say, "I can't!"

Here is a Pea-ma and Pea-pa
with hair that's turned grey.
They sprinkle goodnights and

"I love you," they say.

And look at this pea
with a baby lima bean,
Who grew in his mom's
heart and not in her belly
very different in look,
but a perfect match

like peanut butter and jelly.

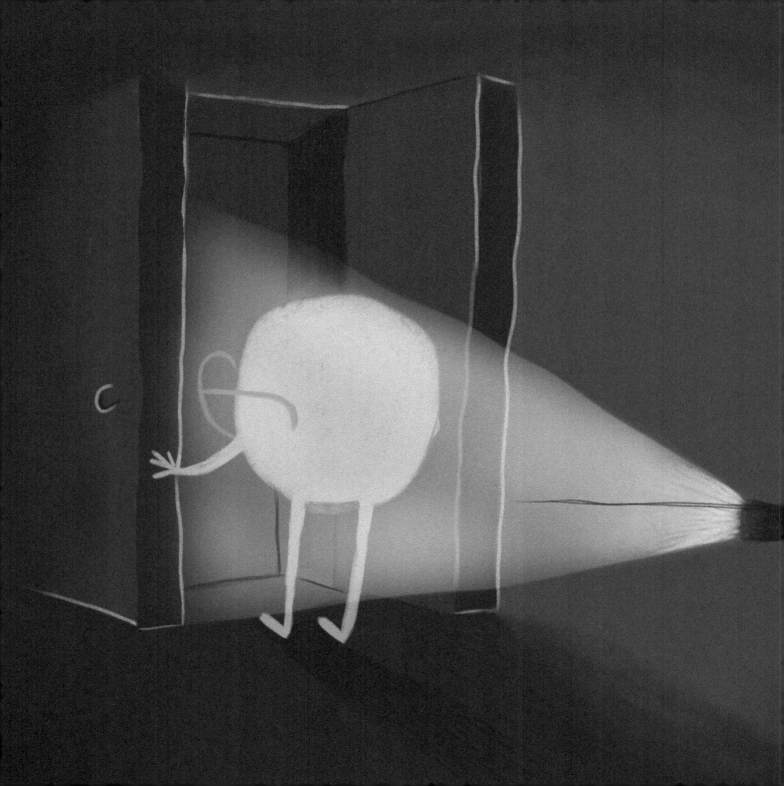

This little pea is with her foster family.
They may not look alike,
but their hugs are just as tight and
they check the house for monsters
when it's time to say goodnight.

This little pea has two
where you may only have one.
But having two pea dads is

twice the fun,

with so much dad love
for their little pea son.

Here is a step mom
and half siblings.
The bigger the crew
is more love and pea-ple
to be there for you.

And then some little
peas have siblings
who learn fast.
Some little peas
have siblings
who learn different.
Some little peas
may use a wheelchair,
wear glasses,
or have boo boos
in a cast.

But ALL little peas
when tickled
start to laugh.

See little pea,
all that can be
when love is the glue
connecting you to me.
See little pea,
there's no need to feel blue,

what completes a loving family

is little pea, you!

THE
END.

CREATE YOUR OWN PEA FAMILY

Cut out:

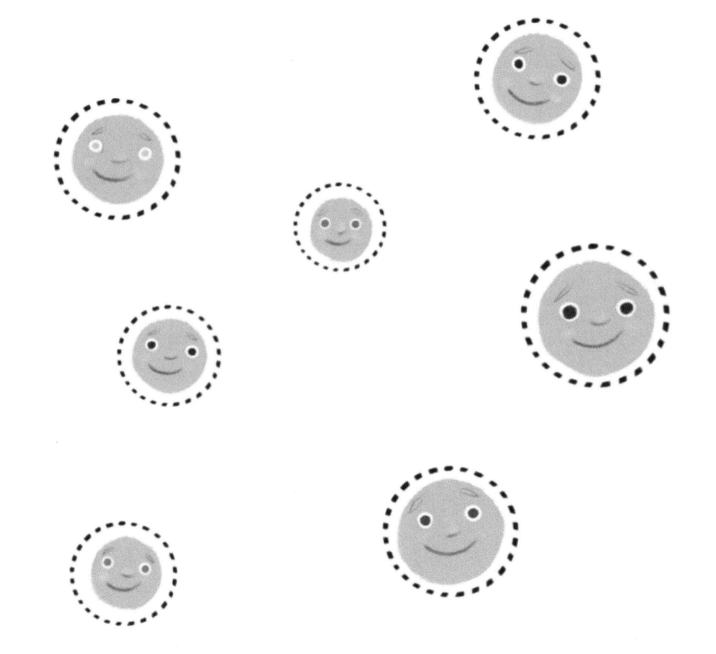

Accessories:

Accessories:

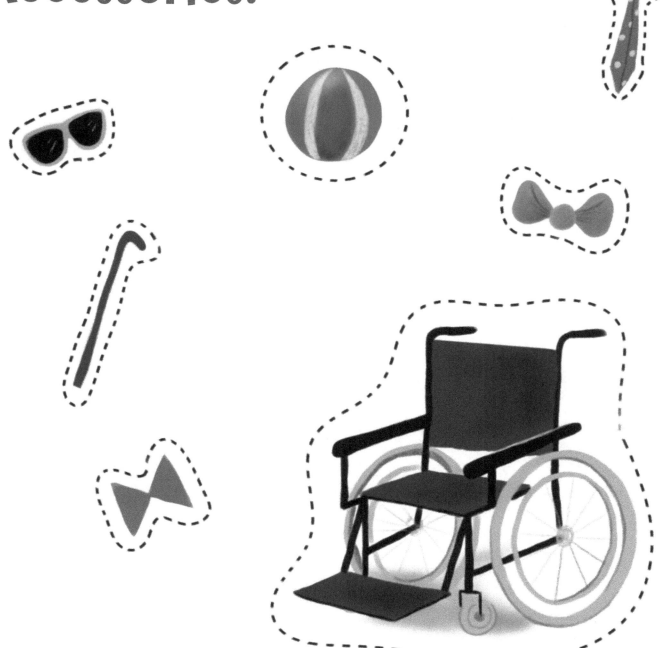

About the Author

Melissa Mangiapanella is a poet, writer, and author of the new children's book *Pea-ple of the World*. As a professionally trained writer and educator, Melissa has spent the last decade creating educational content to elicit cognizance of life-skill fundamentals, such as inclusion. Melissa has a MFA in English and a MFA in Special Education from Molloy College, as well as a BFA in Journalism from Adelphi University. Melissa's love for poetry has led her to travel abroad for enrichment courses and to study under other published authors and poets as well. Melissa has been a lifelong writer and first began creating poems at six years old.

You can reach Melissa at melissadmangiapanella@gmail.com

Illustrator Contact

vitf29@gmail.com

CPSIA information can be obtained
at www.ICGtesting.com
Printed in the USA
LVHW061101271020
669932LV00003B/37